# What's the Time Mr Wolf?

Written by
**Lucy M George**

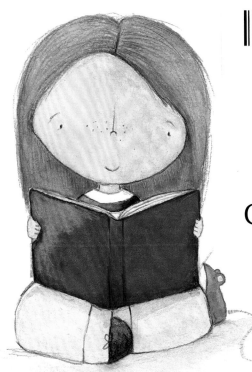

Illustrated by
**Gemma Raynor**

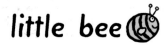

little bee

Lauren sits beside her Grandfather listening to the **ticks** and the **tocks** that sound all around. A twitchy little movement catches her eye.

# A mouse!

Jones' Clock Shop

Closed

Lauren stands up
and runs after it.

"Don't be long!"
Grandfather calls.

"It's nearly..."

...but she's
gone.

Lauren follows
the Mouse to the biggest,
oldest Grandfather Clock
in the whole room, so big
she can't even see the top,
so dusty it doesn't
**tick** or **tock**
like the other clocks.

Lauren reaches
up and pulls
the immense
door open.

# A ladder!

Lauren stands on her tiptoes
and peers up into the darkness
then begins to climb.

Up and **up**

until she can't even
see the floor
below.

**Up** and **up**

towards a light until…

Lauren enters an enormous bright room
full of hundreds and thousands of books,
which spread out in every direction.

Lauren pulls a book off the shelf
and carefully opens it
and reads the first page
out loud…

"What's the time
Mr Wolf?"
she says.

Her voice echoes out
into the silence.

"It's seven o'clock,"
growls the Wolf.

"Time to get up!"

Lauren thinks about this.
"It's not seven o'clock," she says.

**"And I'm already up!"**

So, she asks him again,
**"What's the Time
Mr Wolf?"**

"It's nine o'clock," he growls even louder.

"Time to go to school!"

Lauren thinks about this again. "It's not nine o'clock," she says. "It's not time to go to school!"

So, she asks him again, "What's the time Mr Wolf?"

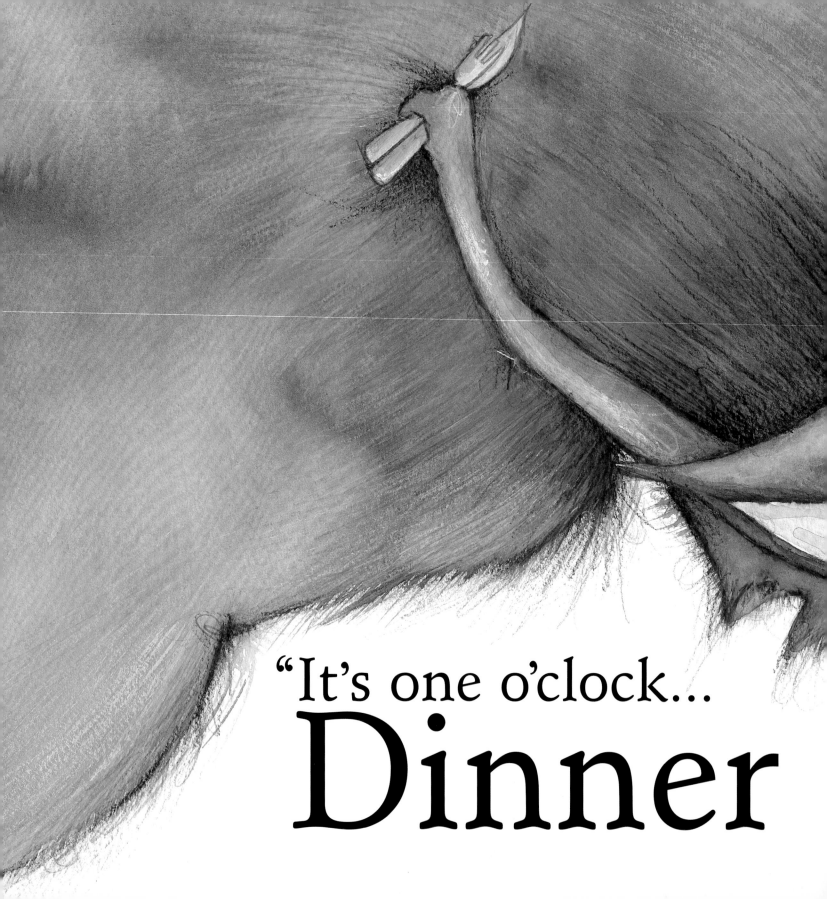

"It's one o'clock...
Dinner

time!

Lauren drops the book,
which falls down,

down,

down,

all the way
to the floor below.

She starts down the ladder,
faster and faster and faster,
towards the ground.

The Wolf is after her!

As Lauren reaches the open book
lying on the dusty floor,
she looks up and the Wolf is

# right behind her!

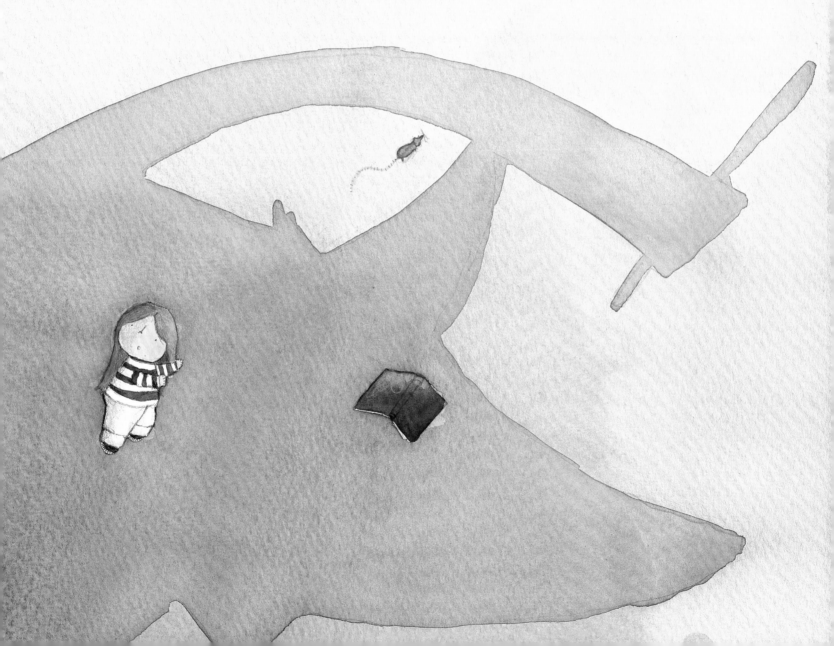

She picks the book up
and, with a smile,
## slams it shut!

And the Wolf disappears
in a puff of dust!

"What are you doing
in there Lauren?"
comes her Grandfather's voice
from the front of the shop.

"Oh, not much," she replies.
"Only reading!"

"Well hurry along now," he calls,
"It's one o'clock...

# Dinner time!

This edition published 2009 by Little Bee, an imprint of Meadowside Children's Books
First published in 2007 by Meadowside Children's Books, 185 Fleet Street London EC4A 2HS
Illustrations © Gemma Raynor 2007
The right of Gemma Raynor to be identified as the illustrator has been asserted by her in accordance with the Copyright, Designs and Patents Act, 1988
A CIP catalogue record for this book is available from the British Library
10 9 8 7 6 5 4 3 2 • Printed in China